Destroy Creation

Destroy Creation

A NOVEL IN VERSE BY

RYAN A. KOVACS

PHiR Publishing
San Antonio

PHiR Publishing
San Antonio, TX
phirpublishing.com

First edition: November 2023

ISBN: 979-8-9885651-1-6
Library of Congress Control Number: 2023915057

Printed in the United States of America

This book is dedicated to my wife, Emma. This was the closest thing to a love story that I could write for you. I love you.

DESTROY CREATION

Ryan A. Kovacs

Succession I
Look

"Why do humans feel the urge to destroy?"
Alex asked me gently
while she stroked the long hair down the back of my neck.
Her saddened gaze at the television
displaying hate and corruption
on the evening news was interrupted
"Well, it was Picasso who said
'The urge to destroy
is also a creative urge.'
So, one could conclude
that to destroy is also to create, yes?"
I answered her question with a question.

"When you say it like that
it makes me rethink wanting to have a baby,"
she stated despairingly.

I rolled over
bringing my face to hers
with my lips just inches away
so that the distance my words traveled
would reach her faster than a silent kiss
"It will happen for us in its own time
and when it does
the fear of destruction will be but a shadow
in the light of what we create."

"Do you think there's something wrong
with my body?
I mean
all the chemotherapy…
all the medications…
all the stress…"

I interjected
"Stop.
Just stop.

You worry too much about the things
outside of your control
rather than worrying about the things
within your control."

I leaned in and kissed her forehead
while she pushed her head into the tenderness of my lips
pulling my naked body close to hers.
Within moments our bodies were entwined
like vines wrapping around a tree
our limbs both wild and tamed
as we crawled along each other's skin
tiptoeing as if we would break
but forever embraced by the love that held us together.

It had been 15 years since the incident
and in that time
the trials I faced could never
have prepared me for what I would ultimately
choose to do.

Many times, I fought those inner demons
the voices and words that resonated
like screams in a well.
I felt trapped like a fish in a tank
wondering why I could see
beyond what was before me
but never able to escape my own fate.

That's why the illusion of control
grants so much power.
Because no different than the fish
my surroundings were familiar and comforting.
Yet being stripped of making my own choice
to leave the tank
and swim freely in open water
was the fear I never knew I had.

Until I was
                    alone
in a world
where no one knew I existed.

There was a moment of dedicated time
when I stood atop the burning ashes
of rubble and sand
where grief was but a dagger
slowly being pulled from my heart
that I realized all I had loved
was now lost.

My father
who bravely took the chance to warn me
sacrificed his life to allow me a choice
and in that
I chose not to be what they wanted me to be.
But the consequence seemed more complex
when I asked myself
'what now, do I become?'

Laying there next to Alex
trapped in a lover's gaze
gave me more purpose than I'd ever known
and only begot the answer to my question
to become the only thing, I yearned to be—

a father.

To retrace the past is often similar
to reading a hidden treasure map
where dotted lines make a trail
towards a location unknown
ending at an 'X' that marks the spot.
But my life was no map
and certainly, held no treasures
with a path that only ever led to demise.

Between denial and grief
that outlined my reality
I did the only thing reactive
that my body could recognize
and ran.
The adrenaline that pumped through my body
made me press on throughout the desert heat
forcing me to wither away the pain
that trickled like rain off a leaf.
It felt like a lifetime since I'd seen or felt the sun
smelling air that hadn't been pumped through vents
tasting my own salty sweat from my upper lip
or hearing the rolling wind brush against my ears.

Most of what I did in the coming days after the incident
was hide and survive.
I had little knowledge of what the world knew about me
nor if anyone would be looking for me
until the radios and televisions spoke of
an underground nuclear test that had gone terribly wrong.
They spoke about multiple casualties
a demolished facility
and new nuclear testing
but nothing about me.

It was as if
I no longer existed
and the government believed
I fell victim to the explosion like everyone else.

In turn, I did the only thing I could think of
and started over.
I paid close attention to the narrative
listening in on the stories they told
about underground nuclear testing
and how the incident at Storax Sedan
was a shallow nuclear test that was conducted
at the Nevada National Security Site
on July 6, 1962, as Operation Plowshare.
They claimed that
the program was to investigate
the use of nuclear weapons for
mining
cratering
and other civilian purposes—
whatever the hell that meant.

They warned that the radioactive fallout from the test
would contaminate United States residents
and that it was the *price of science*.

Their warning should have been labeled a promise
as my guilt overwhelmed me
when it became clear
what I'd done to so many people.
To top it off
they honored the fallen
and cursed me by naming
The Sedan Crater
as the largest human-made crater in the United States.

Little did they likely know
it was literally
human-made…

The 320-foot deep
and
1,280-foot-wide crater
was a direct reflection of the impact
I had on the earth.
      Most men only ever measured
      2 ½ by 8 feet.
But I didn't feel any bigger or smaller
than the actualization that clogged my mind
as to the meaning behind it.

I spent more time than I can count
trying to fix what I'd broken
but without exposing myself
and my abilities

    I chose exile.

The contemplation of
self-preservation
or self-destruction
seemed less complicated at the time.
When all I really wanted was
to fall into an abyss of self-pity
and worthlessness
that would hopefully turn itself into the kind of loathing
that brings on damaging thoughts of death.
Yet, whenever it came to survival
it always seemed to be me left standing.

Where we get lost in our thoughts
I think, becomes our reality.
It was as if those many months in captivity
had dissolved like coffee in water
and what blended to form a taste of realism
was but a sip of some dream I'd procured in my head.

However, my reality never changed.

What had changed though, was my mindset.
Something happened to me on a profound level
when I detonated in the facility.
I went from lobotomized lab rat
to stupefied human being.
It was as if the elements of control over me
diminished with my ability to heal and stand victorious
over all who tried to condemn me.
Like starting a new page of a book I'd not yet written
every step I took forward
was one step further
from the past I would attempt to forget.

And so, I started to live my life.
Finding my place in a desolate world
I knew almost nothing about.

Destroy Creation

Initially, my early travels in finding a way to survive
alongside self-discovery were simpler times.
The first week I managed to live off
a small donut shops' waste in their back alley.
Each night they threw away perfectly good donuts
that barely had the day's scent crusted over top of them
yet, they managed to cook fresh ones every morning at 5a.m.
It was every kids' dream I imagined
to live on such a lavish diet of sugar and dough
until I'd been discovered by the owner
who began asking questions that made me nervous.
I grew increasingly suspicious towards the man
as my paranoia kicked in
that I pushed him aside
and ran once more towards the unknown.

It wasn't until I landed myself in a rundown silo on a farm
just a few miles outside that town
before I was greeted with a double barrel shotgun in my face.
I awoke with eyes immediately crossed
staring at the bead
on the tip of the crease between the barrels.

A boastful voice erupted from the shadowy figure
whose face was blackened by the sun shining in my eyes
"What ya doin' on my farm, boy?"
Quick to respond I stuttered
"I…I was looking for some work.
The heat got to me though
so, I figured I'd take a rest."

With the shotgun still in my face he demanded
"Let me see your hands."
I picked them up from the dirt
placing them just above my head
showing him my palms
"Mmhmm," he murmured under his breath
lowering his weapon to his side
"Ain't never seen the handle of a tool have ya?"
I shook my head in disappointment
"I'll give ya a week.
If you don't want to quit by then because of your calluses
I'll pay you a decent wage."
Quick to my feet I patted off my stolen overalls and tan tee
"I appreciate it, sir."
He looked on at me a bit perplexed
"Live around here?"
"No, sir," I responded unwavering.
"Where you plan on staying then?"
"I don't mind the ground much."
He chuckled lightly
then turned his back and began to walk towards his house
"Come on now,
I got eggs, bacon, and hash browns for breakfast.
Work is in forty."

Following him up the porch steps and into his farmhouse
he rested his shotgun against the door frame
before heading into the kitchen.
There, he lit the gas stove throwing a skillet atop the burner
and asked how I liked my eggs.
"Any way you do them, sir."
He looked over his shoulder with a raised eyebrow
"You're a little too polite, son.
Who taught ya your manners?"
There was hesitation in my voice prior to my lie
"My parents, sir."
"And where are they now?"
He placed a few strips of bacon into the pan
while they began to sizzle.
"Dead," I said sternly.

He shrugged the answer off as if he'd anticipated it
before turning to the countertop
pulling a knife from the drawer
while he began to chop up two potatoes.
His fine chopping skills indicated his precision
as he left long strands
of potato like strings after each slice.
Flipping the bacon with a fork
he studied the sounds of the fat crackling like a fire
before he spoke once more
"You got a name?"
A small part of me had concerns
whether or not to be honest
but I pushed myself towards truth and responded
"My name is, Thomas."

With sincerity he spoke lightly
"I'm sorry about your parents, Thomas."

Like a freight train of emotions
his condolences struck at the right moment
and for the first time in as long as I could recall
I felt deep sorrow about my parent's death and my reality.

He saw it in my face
yet still maintained his composure while he cooked
placing the bacon onto a plate
and into the oven to keep warm
as he tossed the stringy potatoes
into the bacon fat-lathered skillet
adding a dash of salt and pepper to the starchy food.
"When my son passed a few years back,"
the man started
"I'd lost my only helping hand around the farm.
Wife died when my boy was young…"
he paused for a moment
stirring the potatoes to help them soften—
perhaps, even his heart too, before finishing his story.
"Never had much in this life to be honest.
What good I did have was with the misses and my son—
but life had other plans."
He leaned over the counter reaching for a bowl
plucking out a few eggs that he cracked over the skillet
cooking them atop of the browning hash browns
before he scrambled it all up into a stuffing-like concoction
letting it simmer for a minute as he continued.
"My son told me once that
the beauty in death
is that life goes on.
Didn't much get it until he passed
before I realized that
regardless of how many people die in this world
life goes on…
and here we are, proving his point."
He emptied the contents of the hot pan
onto the plate before me
and forked two pieces of bacon on top of the hot meal
that he retrieved from the oven

"Forgive my manners, Thomas.
I haven't had company in some time
that I forgot to introduce myself
the name's, Steven."
He glanced at the wall clock behind me ticking
"Now eat up
we got to strengthen them hands there
to make sure you don't quit on me by week's end."

Work on the farm didn't much feel like work
not that I had any actual work experience
but it beat being tortured and manipulated daily.
Sometimes the things Steven would say
reminded me of Dr. Larson and the lessons we shared.

While our relationship was in some ways
an open book
Steven and I didn't talk much in the sense of conversation.
He spoke mostly about
how to do things around the farm
how to hold certain tools
how to tie knots
how to start tractors
how to be better than I was…

"You don't talk much do ya, Thomas?"
"Don't know what to say usually,"
I said thoughtfully.
"Well, words do often escape me too
but it's no excuse to not use them,"
he stated quizzically.

I kept my eyes on the task at hand
but followed the notion
"I have a…
complicated past."

"No such thing as a simple one.
But you can guarantee it
we all got one."

"How did you get over your past though?
I mean
your wife and son died   "
I caught myself speaking without thinking
grinding my teeth and lips together before speaking softly
"…I'm sorry. I didn't mean…"
Steven interrupted

"It's fine.
It's a hard pill to swallow when I hear it aloud
but it's my reality—
I accept that."
He gathered his thoughts for a moment
as he stopped hoeing.
Resting his crossed arms atop the wooden stick handle
he gazed out across the vastness of his potato crops
"You got to remember the four L's
to conquer and overcome your past:

Look—Lock—Learn—Leave."

He removed his hat
and proceeded to wipe his forehead with his handkerchief
as he began to dig once more
speaking between breaths.
"We first must look at the past
analyze it, determine what was good and bad
separate instances like puzzle pieces
before we put it all together and call it 'the past'.

Then we must lock the past
in the past.
It's not part of our present
and shouldn't hinder our future
so, it must remain where it is—
simple as that.

Once we identify it as our past
is when we can learn from it.
Decipher what things we can take from it
to help mold us into the person we desire to be
and have those traits become our character.

Finally, like Newton's Third Law
we must leave the past behind.
The lessons it taught us
the struggles we endured
and the emotions we overcame
were the building blocks towards our destiny.
Once that path is laid out
we must walk it and never look back.

In the end
we need to understand our past
so we don't fear our future."

"Hey.
Where are you right now?"
Alex asked eagerly.
My distant stare was not subtle to her
as she locked eyes with me.
I shook off my gaze
and mustered a smile
"I'm right here with you."

She let out a small chuckle under her breath
"You do realize you're the worst liar, right?"

"That's only because you see through me,"
I contested.
I sighed with faint relief
pulling myself from then to now
being present in a moment we would share
that felt more intense with each one that passed before.

There was a significant connection between Alex and me.
One that stretched beyond
the physical or emotional connections
often perceived by ordinary couples.

Each moment in our life is significant
no matter how inconsequential it may seem.
Yet, our perception of what life should be
does not equate to what life is.

Perhaps that is why I found comfort in the solitude
working on Steven's potato farm.
The world seemed small there
and for a while it was
as he and I worked daily
saying little
thinking more
and like all thoughts
they fester and squeeze their way out of silence
until no different than me
do they explode.

At night I would sit and listen to the radio
praying to myself that nothing about me would be said.
In secret I would often repeat
Dr. Larson's trigger words with a whisper
wondering if I could ever tame myself
let alone put myself under total control
with the full sequence.

I spoke softly
"Head. Boulevard. Six. Park. Right. Flower. Worn. Ciao."

And nothing.

I'd repeat it over and over
waiting for the smallest inkling of evidence
to support my crazy delusions of self-control.

Back at the lab, when my father was killed
I had experienced a level of discipline I'd never done prior
which was the only reason I had escaped.
Yet, it made me question everything I knew about myself
and what I might be capable of.

Night after night I posed questions to myself
as if I were torturing my own damn mind
scaling both a topless mountain and bottomless pit
having no recollection on how
but never failing to understand why.

One evening it registered with me
through a profound conversation with Steven
what 'the past'
                        is
and what it
                        means.

I constantly recalled life altering events
or character defining moments of my past as such
when in reality
each moment that passed was considered
to be part of that tense.

"In the French language
they have the same tenses of speech
that we do in English
yet they have an additional one for the past tense
called Passé Composé,"
Steven spoke, breaking silence on the outside porch.

"What does that mean?"
I inquired.

"Well, it's mostly used to express
an action or actions that
have or even possibly have not finished
at any point of time, in the past…"
He paused for a moment
formulating his final thought
"I suppose it suggests that, while indeed
the actions of the past are solidified in that tense
or that point in time
our current past is unfolding no different than our present
at a rate that is both unpredictable
and unfinished.
The past, is simply
always growing
and although we cannot change it
the ability to reflect on it

congruently affects the applied lessons towards our future
that can and will alter our past
as it unfolds."

He stared out across his prideful crops
with the smallest of smiles
while we sat there inside our own contemplations
letting silence do the heavy lifting
of some things you just can't explain.

Only a few weeks had gone by
working on the farm with Steven
and while I knew he was curious about me
he was never one to persist.
I felt safe with him and determined it was time to open up
the way he taught me through his compassion.

One afternoon when we were far out in the fields
taking a water break
I began to explain
"I'm sorry I haven't offered much of an explanation
as to who I am and where I'm from.
I've lived some time in both isolation and fear of myself
and what I could do that would harm others."

Steven chuckled mildly
"Thomas, you're a string bean!
What could you possibly do to harm someone?"

I reached into my pocket
and withdrew a piece of paper
with the trigger words scribbled on it.
Handing it to him I exclaimed in as stern of a voice I could
"I'm responsible
for the nuclear explosion of the Sedan Crater."

Steven unfolded the piece of paper perplexed
"What is all of this, Thomas?
These words don't make any sense.
You don't make any sense!
That crater was just some underground testing
that went wrong.
How could you be responsible for that?"

"I want to show you
but I don't know what will happen,"
I hesitated to continue speaking
before I conceded
"I just don't want to hurt anyone anymore."

"Tsk, how will this hurt me?
Or you?
What do either of us benefit
from whatever it is you wish to show me?"
Steven asked wholeheartedly.

"I just want to know if I have control…
to know that I have a choice…"

I began to break down
and rather than pass judgment
Steven looked on at me with bewilderment and empathy
and extended a heartfelt gesture
pulling my rigid body into his
embracing me as if I were his own flesh and blood.

"Thomas," he spoke softly
while the arid breeze cooled the runny tears on my cheeks
"I don't need to know what you've done
or think you've done
just so long as you're safe and happy.
I see that wherever you come from
isn't a place worth going back to."
He sighed before confessing
"I'm a selfish man
taking you in the way I have
out of self-preservation.
You're underage and by all means
I should've reported you to the police
to get you into foster care
but I didn't have the heart."
Releasing his arms from around me
he grabbed my pointy shoulders and pulled my body slightly
blocking the sun behind me with my shadow on his chest
"I'll have you for as long as you wish to stay.
I'll protect you and keep you safe
I promise."

Then he shoved the piece of paper into his overall pocket
drank his water
and we continued with the day's work.

The summer months settled on the farm
while the sunrise and sunsets blended into fall
as if what I'd been doing was what living was all about.
Steven and I sat at the dinner table
going over bills and money made from the farm.
"It just wasn't a good season I suppose.
Lost half the crops even with clear weather.
I wonder why?"
Pausing for a moment to think aloud
"Must be something in the soil,"
he answered himself quickly.
Looking on at me
"I'm sorry I won't be able to pay you much
going into the winter season."

"Your home and cooking will do just fine,"
I stated earnestly.

He smiled gently
as if invisible weight were released from his conscious.
"I've been meaning to ask you
with the new school year approaching
would you like to continue your education?
I can go to the town and see what strings I can pull
and we may have to fudge some paperwork
but a young man as bright as you are
deserves the opportunity to expand that brain."

I hesitated initially before speaking
"I would love the opportunity
I just don't know if I can be around others."

"I see no reason that you can't be around others, Thomas
you have been fine around me,"
Steven retorted.

"I'm good with someone in an individual setting
just, unsure how I'd be with so many others,"
I resisted.

"Does it have something to do with these words?"
He reached into his back pocket
withdrawing the paper that I'd given him with my trigger words.
I stared at it in fear
pleading with him,
"Please, don't say the words.
Not in here.
Not now."

I pushed myself away from the table
backing up in a hurry
"I don't know what will happen,"
I trembled.

"Calm down, Thomas.
I understand your fear and don't wish to force you
into a situation you're uncomfortable with.
But can you explain what these words mean?
Because from my perspective
they are random words with no meaning."

I took a deep breath
inhaling my overwhelming fear
attempting to still my mind
"I can only explain them as words
to both control and unleash me.
The last time I heard them
was the first time I had control of my powers
but I don't know if I still do
and I'm afraid to find out,"
I confessed.

Steven looked both confused and curious
"How long do these *'abilities'* last for?
What do they do?"

I did my best to describe the sequence of events,
"They are kind of like, inside me
locked away until I hear the words
which then gives me the ability to use them at my will.
There doesn't seem to be a time limit
they just kind of, go dormant after a while."

Steven stroked the chin hairs on his graying beard
"Can we go outside to the field
so that I can see what you mean?
This is both hard to understand and believe."

"On one condition—
that whatever happens
you promise not to think differently of me
or tell anyone about me
for both our sakes.
And if it looks like I'm about to lose control
run as far away from me as possible."

"I promise, Thomas."

Dusk was at our backs walking out into the dusty field
while unpicked rotting potatoes were trampled underfoot
with illuminating stars
navigating our way as they would a sailor.
I caught a glimpse of what I presumed to be a shooting star
watching it silently ignite in the midnight blue sky
arcing like a rainbow as its tail blended into the backdrop.

Steven's farmhouse was a small shimmer on the horizon
as I did an about face before him.
I could feel myself quake internally
yet on the outside I remained calm as a clam
ready to open and reveal my pearl of ruin.

I breathed deep and closed my eyes
almost seeing the night sky
painted perfectly behind my eyelids
"I'm ready."

"Head…"

he rehearsed aloud
and like being bathed in fire
Steven spoke the first word
in such a fashion disguised as a familiar voice
that my eyes clenched like fists.
I came to the immediate conclusion
that my fears were true—
I still didn't have any control
and certainly not enough
to tell Steven to stop…

"Boulevard…"

the journey up
the internal mountain had begun
climbing steps and cascading stones
where I would end up
was anyone's guess besides my own.
I was being hurled through a time warp
that begot flinching and motor reflexes to halt
as neurons fired in my brain
like automatic machine guns…

"Six…"

I was a rock sinking in the ocean
plummeting in a downward spiral
with gravity pushing me deeper into darkness
while light escaped above
until I was driven into
the earth's crust like a comet…

"Park…"

blood pulsating with the beat of my heart
ebb and flowing
within caverns of my muscles and joints
that had their own memory
of pain and suffering…

"Right…"

recollections began to collapse
as past images scattered throughout my mind
like a movie reel unchanged
rotating along plastic rivets
that flapped with every rotation…

"*Flower…*"

heat began to build around me
with dirt glassing over
and my anger drawing from a depth within
that seemed to pull with it
an eruption of sheer will…

"Worn..."

like slowly revving up an engine
my peak had nearly been reached
as I not just filled with raw force
but overflowed with it...

"Ciao…"

the conclusion had reached an inevitable end
unleashing a bubble of energy
outward in every direction
and a beam of light towards the sky
igniting the flame
and unshackling the beast within.

I stood there
demonic in nature to the timorous eyes of poor Steven
who was stuck in his stupefaction.
There was little I could offer
to navigate him through his experience
that even I
had no inkling of what I must've looked like to him.
He shuddered with widened eyes as he spoke
"Wh…what… what are you?"

There was no simple answer besides tell him the truth
"I'm the first human atomic bomb,"
I declared.

Steven blinked rapidly like a camera shutter
as if taking still shots with his mind's eye
trying to process all the data he'd been shown
to conclude what he'd say next.
But words escaped him
as did his breath
while he dropped to both his knees clenching his chest
staring into me the way a dying man would
just before revealing the one who'd betrayed him
holding a dagger drenched in blood.
Except I had committed no such crime
besides show him what I'd known
he was not ready to see.

There isn't always beauty in the eyes of the beholder
and it was apparent while Steven struggled
to maintain life moments after my revealing
in which he must've battled with
what was more accepting

                    my birth
                    or his death.

Before I could run to his aid
the compelling irony of all I'd bore witness to in my life
was the simple acceptance that Dr. Larson
had been right all along about my inevitable destruction.

In what way was I part of this tragedy that was my life
and the lives of all those who I'd come to know?

Destroy Creation

Kneeling beside Steven
who silently suffered from an apparent heart attack
living out his last few seconds looking at me
reached for my hand and held it
acknowledging what I presumed
was an unspoken message that his death was not my fault.
But it did not make me feel any less responsible
for having brought it on.

While his final breaths slipped away
I confessed to him the loss of my parents and unborn sister
the men I'd killed in the underground facility
and the revenge I'd taken out on Dr. Larson.
Steven was my diocesan Cathedral
being ears that I hoped would hear my pain beyond the grave
with it being the first and only time
I'd explain my origin aloud.
By the time I'd concluded my story
the moon had risen above the horizon
shedding pale light as a clouded sun would
with my shadow cast upon his still warm body
revealing to me a misery I did not want to share in.

I stood in contemplation
outlining all possible outcomes and choices
from which none were appealing.
It appeared that nothing I would choose
would make life any easier
and with almost certain condemnation of my discovery
concealing my identity was the only logical answer.
Exile would not suffice in this growing world
and yet blending in and taking refuge
with another widow seemed unrealistic and unreasonable.
My only option was foster care
disguising my abilities and being forced into a fire
I surely knew would burn
was but my only recourse.

So, I ran away once again.
Forever trying to outrun a past that was faster
a present that was slipping
and a future clouded by uncertainty.
Every step I took forward
felt as though I were walking backwards
while time gripped me in such a way
of a loving friend I'd lost contact with
and picked up precisely where we'd left off.

Yet it felt as though no one would have me.

Broken hearts are more easily mended
than souls without purpose
and with that I determined I must shut the world out.
There was no happy ending for me
no light at the end of the tunnel.
I was an insatiable vacuum that swallowed all goodness
and excreted only death.
My purpose wasn't to fulfill
but to repeatedly fill and empty.

That is of course
until I met
        her.

Succession II
Lock

Bridging the gap of time
from my teenage years in foster care
to a young adult living on my own and fending for myself
would be no different than attempting
to close the gap of the Grand Canyon.
While intriguing as that feat may appear
my time growing up and learning the ways of this world
were the same as casting a stone
into that gaping wound
of the earth's crust.
I kept my head low
making no attempts at friendships or attachments
waking each day with the purpose to wake the following.
Those years would best be defined as a loop
in which I cannot recollect
a single moment that stood out with importance
until the Cuban missile crisis.

While little time had elapsed since Steven's sudden passing
and I was just finding shelter in my first foster care
the news of Cuban nuclear missiles
brought a reality to the United States
that had since been forgotten—
                                        threat.

Those days were impossible to live freely in
and begged for survival with doomsday looming.
Yet I did not feel the same level of fear
that much of the population must have
because it appeared to be that moment
Dr. Larson had prepared me for.
I could have been the bomb the U.S. could send undetected and
swiftly conducted the deeds of the government
while never being blamed.
But when nothing happened
and negotiations seemed to work
I questioned my existence and filled with regret.

The Cold War
was the coldest war we ever fought.
Being frozen
hovering above a button that could
erase existence as we knew it
and no matter how close
we as a nation and world came
the greatest casualties were not
from foreign advancements
but domestic.
It was the war of whispers and conspiracies
the war of words and intentions
that sprouted both determination and fear.

Shortly following the incident of The Sedan Crater
the Limited Test Ban Treaty was enacted.
However, its true motive
was far from protecting innocent lives.

No different than when they studied
the men and women of the Manhattan Project
without their knowledge or consent
the treaty was merely a hidden agenda
to monitor the effects of radiation fallout
in surrounding areas.
Over the course of a decade
those who were affected by the fallout
were compensated with monthly checks
and terminal diseases.

It was the government's way of saying
"I'm sorry. Fuck you."

There were some who received more severe penance—
those who lived under the guise of flowers and rainbows
freely living while freely dying quicker.

The shame in it all boiled down to trust:
trust in the government
trust in thy neighbors
trust in the intentions of all men
only to unveil
those truths as lies.

Some saw through it
the rest just accepted it
but no one ever tried to change it…

they just took the finger as a gesture
issued by the men with power
as an act of peace
and not of war.

Alex got the middle finger at the age of   6
when she began her first treatments for Leukemia.

Again, when she was   13.
At   21
she underwent chemotherapy for thyroid cancer
which was at the same time I met her.

She was, back then, just a survivor.
She claimed her will to live
had burned out with the candles
when she turned   22
and was only given two months to live.

She had the illusion of hope
that was no different than a well you throw a stone in to
waiting only to hear the crashing of water
to have the enlightenment that it wasn't endless.

I was a clinical technician at the cancer clinic
where she received her treatments
and found I could put my rather
useless skill set of emitting radiation out
in an environment where I would not be noticed
and used for some good.

When I penetrated her vein
starting the infusion
she grabbed my hand.
It was chilled like she'd been holding ice cubes
yet, as soft as a rose petal with morning dew.
She looked off in the distance
and appeared as though she were talking to herself
when she asked aloud
"Do you know how to live with a terminal disease?"
Before slowly turning her face into mine.

"No, how?"
I asked simply
taping the needle to her arm.

"You don't live with it.
You die with it,"
she stated unfeeling.

Turning her head away from me
I witnessed a small tear rise in the corner of her eye
that rolled down her cheek like a boulder on a mountainside.
"Do you know the difference between
living and dying?"
I pressed back.
With no hesitation she responded
"No, what?"

"Breathing."

She inhaled deep
and retorted
"This air smells like death."

"How'd you like to get fresh air sometime then?"
I asked coyly.
Gripping my hand tight
she forced a smile
"That would be nice."

Our first date was not full of zest
nor compliments beyond the attire worn by us individually.
Rather, we spoke about the present times we were living in
the changes of the world
our country and its continued turmoil.

Alex confided in me with a profound look of fear on her face.
The kind of fear that told a story of her past
she believed she may never share again.
Amid her angst and disgust for being the recipient
of a cruel and unusual hand
filled with
broken dreams
unwillingness to find joy
and hopelessness in being cured
she opened mildly inside her defenseless demeanor
"All I ever wanted was to be a mother,"
she sighed.
"My mom,"
she tittered quietly
"My mom was so incredible.
We didn't have it all
but I tell you
she gave it all.
All her love and all her affection…
her precious time.
Gah, she'd read me bedtime stories
and give unique voices to each character
just to make it more believable and entertaining."
She paused for a moment
as if hearing her mother's voice in her head.
"She's the reason I wanted to be a mom
so that I could do all those same things with my kid
and love them unlike anyone else.
To be a part of the miracle that birthing a child is
carrying them for months
feeling them grow inside my tummy,"
she wrapped her arms around her stomach
almost hugging herself as she swayed.

"Then, to bring that life into this world
to hold what was once a living part of you
now living on its own,"
her arms floated outward from her belly
opening as if a child were being placed into them
rocking the air.

Until immediate disappointment ran over her
driving her arms to her sides in a microburst of anger
"But that'll never be me.
I'll never give birth to a child
because all this cancer has done
is destroy my insides
making it impossible for me to conceive."

I let her stay in her silence for a moment before I retorted
"Trust me when I tell you this
nothing is impossible.

I'm living proof of that."

I immediately regretted my statement
after it had been spoken aloud
and much to my surprise
Alex wasn't at all pushy about the meaning behind it.

"What do you mean?"
she asked gently.

I backpedaled in my mind
trying to find an excuse to not tell her my past
nor what I was
"I suffered an accident as a child.
I don't remember much of it
but was told I shouldn't have survived.
Yet here I am
standing before you
alive and well."

She turned from me
likely knowing I was lying
but unseeingly interested
brushed it off on to the next subject matter.

"Why do you work with people who are dying?"
Alex interrogated with a simper.

"I don't see it that way I suppose."
I responded quickly.

"How's that?
Those people have cancer
with no cure.
Their life expectancy is shortened
with death inevitable
and you don't see that clinic
filled with people who are dying?"
She protested with contempt.

"We are all dying the moment we are born
and we spend our whole life trying to stay alive.
I don't see you or anyone else suffering with a disease
as this morbid shell
waiting to empty their life.
My mother had cancer before I was born.
When the doctors told her she had to choose
between receiving treatment and not giving birth
or not receiving treatment and giving birth
with the likeliness of the cancer spreading
she chose me over her survival.
She chose life over inevitable death.

She lived for 10 more years after that.
She didn't survive for 10 more years—
        she lived.
She explained it to me in her final weeks
that to live truly
we must know what it means to lose.
Whether it be a part of ourselves
or someone or something we love boundlessly.
It is not until we lose something
that we realize what to live for."

"So then, what are you living for?"
Alex asked intrepidly.

What answer could I give her that wasn't deceptive?

Truly, the only reason I'd been given to live
was to destroy those who posed a threat
and to be the difference between one or many lives.

I had merely been going through life
living one day to the next
running from a past I prayed was just a dream.
But nightmares like me are never made up
they are simply the sum of all our fears.

I tried another lie
one that supposedly stuck with her when I spoke
"I'm living for the chance to make a difference."

Alex perked up
"That seems as good a reason to live
than any other I can conjure."

And so, it was
a lie I came to believe.

One I tried to force into truth
that would undoubtedly be the very reason
Alex turned to me
and kissed me.

Like lightning
light shot from neurons firing
forcing my eyes shut with wonder
as to why.

When she pulled away
her eyes locked with mine as they peeked open
"What was that for?"
I asked stupefied.

"The idea of hope."

"Hope in what?"
I questioned intently.

Alex held back tears
in a state of unprocessed clarity
"Hope that I won't die alone."

I was captivated by her immediate change in heart
and genuinely questioned my thoughts
along with the feeling that rolled over me.

There was so much I wanted to confess
and yet
out of self-preservation and protection for us both
I unwillingly stayed closed
laying each brick of my wall higher and higher
to guarantee no one could get in.

Alex didn't want answers
she wanted meaning—
a purpose.

And don't we all?

Destroy Creation

It didn't take us long
before we started holding hands on walks down the street
phone calls that ran late into the hours of the night
kisses on the cheeks and lips before departing
and a simple phrase that carried with it
the weight of the world.

We shared our first glimpse of love in the car one evening
while the mid-summer breeze
blew through the rolled down windows.
Soft melodies played through the speakers
to the tune of *'Us and Them'* by Pink Floyd
as we star-gazed and dreamy-eyed one another.
The night was close to conclusion
while we spoke profoundly about the song in the background
understanding the dichotomy
within the limits of our own experiences
while secret undertones danced around my mind
to the secrets I wished to reveal.

And yet
we sat there side by side
inches apart feeling conjoined
stuck in the moment that continued to pass
with words that stopped being voiced.

Like a hurricane had swept our thoughts
we each roared the word within our minds
as if shouting from a mountain-top
that would echo through the night.
We sealed our lips
sharing the indistinguishable fear
of pushing one of us away
had we uttered the word of deep affection.

Rather than potentially be denied
we sat there drawing nearer
allowing a fleeting passion
bounce between us
like molecules in a chemical reaction
that would soon overflow and combust
allowing us to feel equally about one another.

It was indeed the first time I had loved
another human being other than my family
and like all things that are loved

I did not want her to leave.

If there is in fact anything I've learned in my lifetime
it is that we are all connected.
We may not know it right away
or sometimes
ever at all
but the world is too small
and life too short
to have everyone in existence be
nothing but matter squeezed and pressed together
not once sharing a fraction of similarity.

Those moments are masked as common expressions
fate—coincidence—destiny—divine intervention
yet, all these chances
we deem as some serendipitous happening
are those small links that continuously bind us all together.

There is no such thing as being alone
no matter how unaccompanied
we perceive that present tense to be.

At least that's what I kept telling myself
knowing full well
there was nobody else in the world
like me.

Perhaps I should have seen it coming
the story that unfolded like pages in a book
as Alex went on about her mother over dinner.
It appeared that her mother
was never removed from her mind
constantly being reminded of a memory
that begged confession
as if defending the fear of forgetting altogether.
I listened intently
hearing her emotional testimony
about the benign, zealous woman she was.

I couldn't tell what the spark was
that ignited such profound recollection
whether it was the proper way she held her fork
or the way she twirled the pasta
or the metal clinks of the prongs on the spoon
before she began to confess
"My mother died from cancer."

I stopped eating
while my mind raced with questions
How?
When?
Why?

But nothing prepared me for what she said next.

"My mother and I were victims
of the Storax Sedan nuclear test.
Are you familiar with it?"

My legs trembled.
I began blinking rapidly
as my breathing intensified
and palms grew clammy.
I had sunk inside myself
while simultaneously thrusting a word from my mouth
"Yes."

She looked back down at her noodles
allowing me a reprieve to collect myself
"It was the largest radioactive fallout from a nuclear test
in the history of the United States.
We didn't know how terrible it would be
and of course, we didn't realize the consequences
until a few years later.
She told me she had cancer when I was 12
that if she didn't make it
the government would take care of me.
They'd already been sending us checks periodically
since we were affected by the fallout
but they never told us how fatal or detrimental it would be.
The only thing I needed was a mother that would live
not some paycheck to keep me silent about a matter
that was never fully explained."

She put her fork down to wipe a tear from her eye
"My mother told me about the news over a pasta dinner
and sometimes I wish what she told me was true—
that after I finished my meal, I'd feel better.
That sometimes we must swallow our feelings
because regurgitated words
that have been churned and digested
don't sound as good coming out as they do going down."

She paused for a brief second
as she continued
"I know you're probably wondering
why I'm bringing this all up.
The truth is, I met with my doctor today
and he said that my thyroid cancer
has become more aggressive
giving me only a few more months to live.
I've chosen to stop my chemotherapy
and live out my remaining days
with you by my side hopefully."

Life may sometimes be both
cruel and unusual
which in turn is mostly ironic
because we condemn that kind of torture
towards those we attempt to punish or kill.

Yet, we don't bat an eye at the subtleties of living
that condone behavior otherwise frowned upon
by those who wish to die.

In that brief moment that Alex revealed to me
that I, was in fact, the one
who had damned her and her mother
my existence felt cursed
and moreover
cruel and unusual.

How was it
that fate or destiny or whatever the fuck you want to call it
allowed our paths to collide
bearing the fruits of love and hope
yet, deplored death and despair
as if already preordained?

It can be argued
that life is more precious than time—
and yet, without time itself
we would not have life.
Funny how the two are interwoven
until they are severed from one another.

I imagine them as one entity until they're divided
creating a gap or a lapse
all of us will eventually fall in to
and never be able to escape.

It was a premature feeling of death that overtook me
as if stuck in a void
where silence muted my screams.

I selfishly spoke with rhetoric to myself
'this must be what dying feels like'.

I battled the demons inside me that sought to emerge
stricken with both fear and anger.

Where was my choice in all the chaos that surrounded me?
Where was the reality that pestered understanding?
Where was the truth amidst the fallacy that is living?

I reached across the table to grasp her hand
lightly stroking her fingers with my thumb
"I'm not going to let anything happen to you,"
I proclaimed.

Sarcastically she retorted
"Then nothing will ever happen to me."

Her smile was full.
She didn't know how serious my proclamation was
that behind it was a vow
to do the one thing I'd not been able to do thus far—

save someone I loved.

Destroy Creation

Without her knowledge or consent
I began to fulfill my promise and keep her alive at all costs.
It was aggressive at first
in an attempt to kill the very thing that poisoned her
while poisoning the poison.

How is it that a cure
can be just as annihilating as the disease itself?

What determines the order of chaos
when the very function of cells in the body
are there to facilitate immunity through impunity
yet are met with deterioration through retribution?

It is just further proof of unpredictability
and the unquestionable admittance
that no one is exempt from consequences.

The price to pay couldn't be calculated
under the cloud of uncertainty
and I risked being known for it.
"I don't want to jinx anything
or even remotely get my hopes up
but lately I've felt different… better almost,"
Alex began to confess.
"I don't know what I would do with good news.
Is that sad?"

"It is,"
I admitted lightly.
"It's sad
because you've been given bad news
almost your entire life.
Manipulated by living
in order to be comfortable with dying.
While I believe we should all find peace with death
it should not be what we look forward to because of a lackluster life."

"I guess I just spent so much time
waiting for the end to come
that everything in the middle got lost in time."
She began to cry
pouring out her emotions no different than her tears
"I don't want you to think
that I have ever taken any moment with you for granted.
What we've had and shared has been
meaningful and purposeful.
I just don't know why I'm selfish to give that all up
because I'm tired of fighting."

"I don't fault you for the notion
nor do I take offense.
We should all be in control of our own destiny
and if you've chosen to let go of that
to let fate, take the wheel
I can't think of a better way to go."
I cleared my throat
signifying importance
                    "A choice is a choice."

She gazed into me with her waterfall eyes
admitting to me
"If by some miracle I survive
will you promise to give me something
I've longed to have?"

"Anything for you."

She declared
                              "I want a family."

Succession III
Learn

What we do with uncertainty
can be dangerous and corrosive.
I say that from the perspective
having lived my life
unknowingly a victim to consequences
that constantly shaped my future.

Alex was not concerned with what was to be
as much as what already was.
In her eyes, the doubtfulness was not a drape of pessimism
but a comforter she'd gotten to know warmth from.
I on the other hand had become borderline obsessed
with controlling the path of hers and my life
that I'd come to know fears of loss that compounded
like dirt being shoveled into a hole.

When we dressed Thursday morning
October 6th, 1975
we both stared into the mirror of our apartment bathroom
with different expressions.
One of hope
one of dread
and both of us right for contrasting reasons.

Slipping on her emerald silk dress
I couldn't help but grin at her benevolence
as she caught my glance in the reflection
"We don't have time
for whatever it is you're thinking, honey,"
she tittered.

"Sorry, love.
You know how I get when I'm anxious,"
I winked.

As soon as the joke was woven
the mood swung back like a pendulum
to the day at hand
and the answers we sought.

The drive to the fertility clinic
felt like a speeding bullet
as I purposely attempted to drive slowly
yet never caught a red light
or had to slow for crossing pedestrians.
It was as though we were a step ahead of time itself
fractions before
moments soon
and instants thereafter.

I watched in the rearview mirror
the former, unfold with all the points in time
that came immediately after
like we were drifting through the present
at the precise speed in which
the future blended with the past.
Before I came to realize the nature of this effect
I'd already begun my left-hand turn
into the parking garage in downtown Salt Lake City.

Engaging the vehicle into park
we each let out a sigh
that sounded louder to the other
as we turned and looked at one another with determination.

"Whatever the news today
I want you to know that I still won't give up,"
I confided.

Her eyes welled for a moment
while she sniffled and drew them back into her eye sockets
"I know you won't.
You never have."

When we entered the clinic
the waiting room was disturbingly empty.
The feeling of despondence
leaked through the curling wallpaper
as I imagined the way
many women before must have felt.

The unseated chair...
the unread magazine...
the unopened door...
the unlit nightlight...
all slightly uncomfortable
for uncertainty's sake.

Selfishly I withheld the correlating notion
and rapidly withdrew the thought
so, to not appear weak
when Alex needed strength.

Of course
when she asked me the night before
if by some happenstance it was her
and all the radiation she'd been subjected to
that had prevented her from getting pregnant
I reverted to my own selfishness
that it could have very well been me
impeding on her ability to reproduce.
The many unbeknown years of
pouring radiation into her body
could be the unpredicted diagnosis
that I would have to take responsibility for.
I vowed to tell her the truth of it all
if her body was found to blame
so that she would not have to live her life with guilt
being unable to give life
while she prevented her own death.

I couldn't comprehend her emotions
while we anxiously awaited our names to be called.
Every tick of the clock
or outside noise erupted from the busy street
made heart palpitations echo like sound through a cavern.

From behind the receptionist desk
a faint tune played from the radio to that of
Pink Floyd's 'Wish You Were Here'.
I honed in on the lyrics
analyzing their dichotomy, the same way I did
the night Alex and I sat in my car
listening to 'Us and Them'.

It felt too ironic
like it was Us…
against Them—
wishing only for a child to be here
with Us…
and not Them.

But life is only poetic through coincidence
and we were
no song titles
no lyrics
nor rhymes.
We were merely a consequence
of what happened
and what would soon be.

"Thomas and Alex,"
the nurse called our names while opening the door.
It swung like the breath it had stolen from Alex and I
exhaling a tense sigh in unison.

We walked back to a study
rather than the typical examination room
where we were met with two red leather-bound chairs
a hickory desk like that of a brick wall
and the doctor who would share the news.

When we sat
each of us slumped into our own comfort zone
engaging defense mechanisms
and questions at the ready.
Armed and guarded with thoughts and feelings
with fear of rejecting the truth
should it not line up with our beliefs.

"Good morning, my name is Dr. Geene.
I'm the fertility Doctor at this clinic
and was handed your file personally."
Flipping through the manilla folder
and rustling paperwork
he shifted some loose leaf
and withdrew a document.
"Before we get into the diagnosis
I wish to confirm that you indeed did undergo
multiple chemotherapy treatments
for diverse types of cancer?"
He directed his question at Alex.
"Yes.
Three separate times."

"Says here, you denied treatment for Thyroid Cancer…"
He looked up from the folder to make eye contact with her.

Alex confirmed simply
"Mmhmm."

"Can you tell me why and what happened?"

She pondered for a moment then spoke up
"I guess you could say that I came to terms with my death.
It seemed like the universe was telling me to die
so, I figured, I hadn't tried it yet."
She paused mid-thought
whimsically recalling
"But I guess the universe wasn't ready for me to die.
No sooner did I get the news I had a few months to live
did I somehow go into remission.
The countless specialists I spoke to could not determine
the cause or reason for my miraculous recovery.
And I have been healthy ever since."

"Do you believe in miracles Miss?"
Dr. Geene asked gently.

"Of course I do.
I am living proof."

"I believe children are true miracles in this world.
The act of conception and fertilization
is nature's true miracle.
I want to believe
that every person should experience such a phenomenon
but sadly, Mother Nature can be choosey.
However, based on your bloodwork
I don't see any dangerous levels of radiation in your body
that would prevent you from conceiving.
The fact that your body has retained any
at this point is a mystery
but not what is preventing pregnancy."

The room seemed to elevate with optimism
with Alex interjecting
"So, what's the problem then?"

The doctor sat back with unease
but responded promisingly
"It's possible it just hasn't taken yet.
I know that's not a comfortable answer
considering you've been trying for some time.
I would however give it a little more time
before exploring other options."

Destroy Creation

It wasn't unwelcomed news to say the least
because Alex smiled and cried
under the light of hope once more.
Her veil was lifted and her acceptance on the matter
could not have been predicted
when the worst was mostly what we had prepared for.

But something inside me
tugged at an unraveling string.
Something about a man of science
speaking like a man of faith
drew me towards a potential lie
set in motion by his influential lips.
The unease was almost palpable
yet I remained calm and collected
to not remove my mask.

We stood to make our exit and Alex lit up
like a star in the midnight sky
as she twinkled and flickered her eyes at me
before laying a juicy kiss upon my lips.
I sank into the happiness that radiated from her face
as her tears touched and ran down my cheek
while we were interlocked.
I removed my doubts just as her
Before she playfully stated
"I hope you're still feeling anxious from this morning,"
winking and pinching my arm.

And just like that
it was better.

All her doubtfulness drowned by confidence
that the hopes of conceiving a child far outweighed
the inability of not being able to.
She turned and started out the door
and before I could take my first step
the doctor's voice spoke up
"Thomas, if I could have quick word."

Alex continued
shutting the door behind her
while I sat back down
making eye contact with Dr. Geene.
There was a moment of silence before it broke like glass
"I wanted to speak with you privately about another matter
in order to avoid confusion or embarrassment.
I'm sorry to say this to you
but Alex cannot get pregnant with you."

I interrupted furiously
"But you just told her that she can get pregnant!"

"She can.
But she can't get pregnant with you…"
he rebutted.

"I'm sorry, what is it that you are implying here?"

"That you're infertile, Thomas."

There's a superficial lie we sometimes tell ourselves
when confronted with the truth—

                                        denial.

It disguises itself as:
No. It can't be. It's not possible. I don't believe it.

It is followed by an overwhelming flood of actualization
as you imagine the truth as a reality
rather than a possibility.
Sinking deeper into the depths of the mind
and what it believes
the mere speaking of the truthfulness
reverberates both a sense of wonder and awe.
Emotions attach themselves
like suturing a wound
to close the veracity
in its own designated space
while finger-like visions of a future
develop into practical outcomes.

Destroy Creation

We cannot control the truths spoken to us
but rather, the ones within us.
It is only through acceptance that we are calmed—
forged from the realm in which thought is created
and used in a manner for which perceptions to destroy.

My truth was
unbecoming
unbearable and
unaccompanied by sensitivity.

Spoken, heard, and felt
all in a single moment
in which a relapse of my own history
was no more important
than a future that no longer existed.

I was created
yet I could not create.
> Nothing was more destructive to my sense of peace
> than being powerless to reproduce in my image.

An overwhelming sense of defeat cascaded over me
as the doctor provided statements and questions.
"I am terribly sorry for sharing this news.
I didn't want to divulge the information before
asking you a few follow-up questions
and ultimately leaving you with the decision
whether or not to tell her."

"Why would I not want to tell her?"

"Forgive me for sounding insensible
but it gives you a way out of your relationship
while not exposing the truth to her..."

"So, you're suggesting I lie to her then?"
I retorted angrily.

"I'm just saying
if you're too embarrassed to admit
and don't want to endure the costs
and giving her false hope
when she is perfectly healthy enough
to have someone else's child..."

I immediately cut him off
"How dare you imply such an inconsiderate outcome.
I've heard enough."

Proceeding to the door
he reached over his desk and grabbed my hand
attempting to hold me back
"Thomas, your blood test came back
with dangerous levels of radiation.
Your sperm count was non-existent
and quite frankly
I don't know that you're helping Alex
by staying with her..."

I clenched my fist
and ripped it from his grasp
before he retracted
wincing from questionable pain.
I shot him a look of confidence upon exiting the room
"We're finished here."

Destroy Creation

I closed the door behind me with force
and was met with Alex's eyes just down the hall.
She invited me with a smile
to which I put on the masquerade
and met her hand with mine as we conjoined fingers
upon leaving the office.

Outside the sun was radiant
and Alex beamed with expectations
of something known and possible.
I managed to keep it all together
despite having reached a height in my existence
I was forced to fall from.
It was decided that this newfound secret
could not be my decision alone
and begged for confession.

I drew out the events in my mind
figuring it best to have the conversation over dinner.
I wanted to celebrate her
since she was no longer in question
and deserved recognition of beating cancer
moreover, beating death on multiple occasions.

"Where to?"
she asked with jubilation.

"How about the nearest florist to celebrate?"
I suggested.

"That would be nice,"
she concurred.
"What did the doctor want to speak to you about?"

Deceivingly I admitted
"He gave me some suggestions on what might help."

"Hopefully you can show me tonight,"
she played, while offering me another wink.

Walking down the street
I stopped at the nearest intersection
in front of a business on the corner
and politely asked the gentleman outside sweeping his entryway
"Excuse me, can you give me directions
to the nearest florist?"

He nodded and responded

    "If you head
   down the boulevard
about six
    blocks, you'll come to a park
   on your right.
     The flower
shop is called 'Thorns to be worn'.
    Ciao!"

Frozen.

Completely and utterly still.

I had succumbed to a notion building within
from which I knew little about.

An absence   now existent.
A past   now present.
An idea   now reality.
A lapse   now continued
from where I left off
in that dusty field next to Steven's dead body.

Words that percolated
and produced an unwelcoming response
to my damnation.

Destroy Creation

Like stepping out of a mold
or shedding my outer most skin
that I spent years concealing
unraveled and fell to my feet
no different than gravity keeping me grounded.

Stuck between what felt like two dimensions
my inability to move like a statue
rose from the earth's core
and bled into me
absolute power.
The words spoken
in the sequential order were like hearing in slow motion
while every other sound was reduced to static.

"if you

                                                              head...

down the

                                                            boulevard...

about

                                                                  six...

blocks, you'll come to a

                                                            park...

on your

                                                              right...

the

                                                          flower...

shop is called Thorns to be

                                                              worn...

                                                              ciao...

My body micro-twitched incessantly
while an invisible aura began to encompass me.
Alex's voice was almost non-existent
while her lips moved frantically.
She extended her hand in an attempt to grab me
but was soon met with boiling heat on her palm
as my radiant energy coursed outward along my skin.

Her pain and dismay
left her facial expression confused yet terrified
until she stepped backwards.
And no different than a familiar time before
it was like watching a scene on repeat
having gathered the images from every angle
while I helplessly witnessed her foot slip off the sidewalk
and she free-fell into the street
where her entire body was struck by a passing vehicle.

The tires screeched and passerby's gasped.
But in the very moment
that I regained control to reach for her
she was already out of distance from my grasp.

The earth stopped spinning
the clocks skipped a second
my soul left my body
in that mere fraction of an instant
that I had lost control.

By the time the vehicle had stopped
Alex laid slain on the pavement
with blood leaking from her skull.
The impact of her body
was that of a meteor crashing into the earth's crust
leaving an imprint on the asphalt and my mind.

Recalling a similar image of my father
who died before my eyes
I blinked like the shutter of a camera
with an overexposed lens to reality
staring at her laying lifeless.

Like Deja vu
I began to come to my senses
in a way both foreign and familiar
that took hold and embraced me
unlike any I'd ever felt.
People approached me attempting to aid
but were met with my overflowing rage.

I sucked out all the air within a fifty-foot radius
onto those who breathed frantically from running
and spewed a plume of radiation outward
choking them within inches of their lives
as they gasped for oxygen
that would not be granted.
Their molecules dissolved under the skin
sending the preponderance to the ground
like undead clenching the concrete.
I stood there
and watched them claw the ground and their chests
clinging to the very thing that was absent
no different than I.

People began to run away in terror
fleeing in every direction
like ants escaping a magnifying glass
while my body ignited
almost catching ablaze
with heat waves elevating my body from under my feet
levitating me above the ground.

I hovered for a moment
emitting a bright yellow glow
absorbing a fierce vitality from within.
I began to push heat ripples from my hands
aiming them at surrounding men and women
boiling them from their insides
as they liquified and burst
into blood red splatters along the ground.

Overcharged and building rapidly
I took aim at parked cars
and pushed them away with force
into buildings and rooftops unabated.
My powers were unlike anything before
while years of suppression refined and made sturdy
all my abilities
but one.

The lack of self-control in those moments
was a misunderstood concept
of failing at absolutism.
I was nothing more and nothing less
than the unchallenged and unequivocal power
that slowly was taking over.

It wasn't long before metacognition set in
freezing my surroundings in a still frame
until I looked back down at Alex
and was met with overwhelming remorse.
In the middle of incomplete dismantling of the city
the human in me sunk back to the ground
gently falling to my knees at her side.

A gust of fresh air found its way into my lungs
and all my senses were restored.
Heightened hearing to screams
and fires in the faraway distance.
Sight to the carnage and damage done
while the smell of engine oil
and smoke erupted in the sky like volcanic ash.

Once again
there I was
confronted with a truth
met with denial
when I asked the universe

why?

"WHY?!"
I screamed to the sky
before sulking into my palms while I pondered how
we condemn the things we know nothing about…

That is until we learn more about the unknown
and the secrets it holds
to then push the limits
agitating boundaries
that inevitably break
opening a gateway to knowledge
we wish we had never discovered.

Perhaps that is why everybody loses at the end of the day.
Some lose gradually
and some all at once
while the idea of winning
is only perpetuated by the ones who know loss
and losing is a consequence winners refuse to adopt.

I had suffered great loss in my life.
Losing every individual with whom I cared for and loved
without ever really understanding the irony.

A voice resonated in the cavity of my mind
whispering to me a forgotten conversation.

"Trial over tragedy, Thomas.
By that I mean
we cannot use our tragedies in life as an excuse
to unwillingly overcome the trials placed before us.
Every person is tested
in the ways for which they need improvement.
That should be our daily drive—
to be better than yesterday.
Sure, there will be times in which we fail
but we must be able to see those failures
for the lessons that they are
as they teach us new ways to change.
I know you are strong enough to endure this program
that Dr. Larson has selected you for
and before you embark on this journey
I just want you to know that I love you and
I am proud of you
for making this selfless decision in your life.
The road has not
and will likely continue
to not be easy for you.
But I am confident that in the end
through all the trials you will face
you will not be a victim of consequence
but a victor of choice."

My father's farewell words to me
before leaving for the program
were a pastime blooming in my present
with a future undetermined
begging for a reply.

I had an obligation to the reality that was before me
that was made up of instances
and within each of them
I died.

This was my truth.
The undeniable pain that overtook my suffering
that led to my creation
and soon
                        to my destruction.

Epilogue II
Leave

An instant.

It is small.
It is fragile.

It is an immeasurable moment of time
that can shape an eternity
define a newness in reality
that otherwise never existed.
Pulling every word ever known
into a singularity like that of a blackhole
encapsulated by unwavering emotions
that create an image
of unimaginable potential.
Within it
births time itself
conjuring matter
beckoning existence
formulating the concept of all actuality.
It was there
that I found understanding
complete control over all things that were outside of it.
Glimpsing at it as if
taking my first breath, pain began to take form within
unlike any before in my life.
It gathered like the ocean tides
pushing and pulling
rolling up and out—
drawing near and far.

    It crept like night crawlers
    inching forward
    paced in survival—
    longing to breathe.

      It built like heat
      rising and raising
      with no cap to prevent spread—
      combusting and igniting.

A cold inferno engulfed me
searing my nerves
severing the connection of thoughts and feelings
until my body was Novocain-incarnate.
Compulsively numb
and bereft of sensation
the depths of my inner most fear
slowly became by outer most reality.

Gripping Alex's body
the heat of her life essence soon began to dissipate
as my external body temperature rose
from Fahrenheit to Kelvin
spreading the radius around me
into dust-like particles.
Waves began to erupt
extending outwards in pulsating movements
burning everything it touched
sinking the earth below
deeper and deeper
revealing myself on a pedestal of land that stood isolated.

Within all the distance I could see
the ground and all its monuments, buildings, and people
scorched and caught ablaze
in a field of desolation
that consumed more than it could possibly devour
regurgitating malevolence.

Destroy Creation

Alex's body began to stiffen from rigor mortis
while my intractable pulses of radiation blew outwards
dissolving her from my very eyes.
Tears were unable to form properly
as they immediately turned to steam upon touching my skin
denying me my internal pain to resolve.
Clenching her draped corpse along the top of my knees
I held on with profound anticipation.
Like being heated from within
her skin began to blacken and crack
crisping as it turned to ash.

Particles floated towards the skies
releasing her remains to the winds that blew her
further and further from me.

And no sooner than when she was alive
she was just a memory.

With nothing but air between my fingers and palms
the actualization of all that had become of me settled.

The calm had arrived
just as it did with every storm before
giving me clarity unlike any lens could see.
With my emotions magnified
the predisposition of fate rested upon my shoulders
like that of a scarf shielding the brisk air.

Unmoved and silent
I rehearsed a pastime that was as palpable as the present
sticking to me like that of sap.

"Thomas, you must understand one concept in your life:
what is, is.
No matter how hard you will try to change or alter
the circumstances of your life
there are constants that cannot be altered.
Hear me now and believe me later when I tell you this—
that the urge to control
is only that, of an urge to lose control.
There will be a time in your life
in which you will be faced with a choice
and while you are being stripped of all choices now
you must always remember
to not make a choice at all
is still choosing to do so.

Now, I do not devise plans
of a future in which you succeed or fail
rather, present those who do make such decisions
a weapon to meet their demands.
Should a day come however
when it is you who faces total annihilation
I hope you'll remember this simple phrase—
the only constant is change.

Thus, you must remain within it
complying to its every request
because the day you choose to disobey it
will be the day the world suffers for your unwillingness
to make a choice."

Dr. Larson's words reverberated through my mind
as if hearing them aloud
while staring off into the desolate distance.
Reconciling his words, I compared his knowledge with Steven's
wisdom when he told me

"I don't know much about a quiet mind
but I know a bit about one that suffers.
If I were a wise man
I would say a suffering mind is often silent
but I would not claim to know anyone other than myself.
Speaking from experience
which is all I have left in life
suggests to me that you are suffering, Thomas.

Now, I don't need to know what from—
that's between you and you.
But you need to confront it…
face it…
because if you continue to push it aside
and treat it like something you can control
the day may come when you can't
and it will be far too late
to resist what it may do to you."

Destroy Creation

While conflicting
I recognized their similarity
no matter how hard I attempted to resist.

It was futile to try and lie to myself
because, behind every lie
is a truth that was once hurt.

I had just lived with it buried beneath layers of protection
with the constant fear of my truth being unleashed.

Yet there I stood
on the edge of cataclysmic devastation
with a choice imploring execution
that I felt inadequate to make.

How fortuitous
that in a life of choice
I chose to deny my purpose…

With every fiber in my being
I had demonstrated the willingness and acceptance
to endure.

A choice not long forgotten
to relinquish all choices henceforth
all brought me to the singular moment of my existence
fulfilling the profound meaning of my life.

Within that moment, I recalled the lesson
Steven learned from his son
and the imperative wisdom it held.

Look.
Lock.
Learn.
Leave.

They were all instances that tied themselves to a pastime
interwoven with the present
that dictated the future.
As fate would have it
the most noteworthy teacher in the equation of life
would singlehandedly be the reaper himself.

What he took without giving.
What he demanded without asking.
What he destroyed without creating.

I was inadequate
and without a doubt
unprepared
to look at my past
and lock it there
all while learning from it
with the intention of leaving it behind.

Now I would be made to suffer the consequences of
my choices.

It was abundantly clear to me
that I was never made to create
for I, was the embodiment of creation itself.

In that singular moment I had proven
that I was not the answer.

Rather, I was the cancer
the planet would be made to suffer from.

Like Mother Nature, I too would be beauty and rage
bringing wrath upon the world
in the form of an event
it would never be allowed to speak of.

It was as Dr. Larson had foretold
when he said he envisioned me
'At the end of it all'.

I stepped forward
readying my body with but one purpose:
to obliterate existence.

I closed my eyes
while the faces of all those I chose to never forget
flickered before me like a movie reel.

Mother—
who chose to birth me.

Father—
who chose to sacrifice for me.

Steven—
who chose to understand me.

Alex—
who chose to love me.

And even Dr. Larson—
who chose to create me…

I leave you all as you are—
as dust from my wake
when I say but one last word to you
which defines who I truly am
and all I will ever do…

"Destroy."

Special Thanks To

My editors, Lois Taubman and Debbie Maier Pavicic for their constructive input.

My artist, Sean Fitzpatrick, for his ability to capture the vision of each book in a singular image.

My publisher, for believing in me and my stories and allowing me to share them with the world.

Acknowledgments

The journey from Create Destruction to Destroy Creation was a culmination of some of the greatest and most difficult life lessons I've come to learn over the years. Additionally, it was also meant to shed light on circumstances that so many people I've come to know over the years have had to endure. Infertility is sadly a larger part of our society now days and yet there is still a stigma that comes with it. It is at no fault of either individual trying to conceive but simply placed in the hands of fate.

I felt that shedding light on the topic along with underpinning themes of choice, control and consequences would help bring understanding to such a sensitive topic. It was through many discussions with friends and family who have had to endure such difficulties that I was able to gain perspective on the subject and found a unique way to express it.

To those who have experienced infertility and those going through it, I hope you always remember that you are never alone with your struggles, and I pray you find comfort and strength in those you confide in.

Lastly, I have been fortunate to have had many mentors in my life. They have brought out in me the very thoughts and feelings expressed throughout each of the titles in the Destruction Series. While cynical, the balance I have had to create in my life is due in part to the lessons I've learned from my past. That would not be possible without those who chose to listen to me while offering their wisdom and advice.

From the very depths of my soul, I give gratitude to the following individuals: Allison Allyn, Joel Blackburn, Athena Desai, Tom Hammel, Brandon Kasperkoski, Julianna (Mama) Kovacs, Bob Ranaletta, Marcus Singletary, Elena VanLare, and Steve Wilson.

About The Author

Ryan Kovacs is the author of *The N.M.E.*, *Create Destruction*, and *Destroy Creation*. Poetic storytelling in verse is his passion, and his philosophical views underlie the stories within each of his books. He resides in Churchville, New York and leads a simple but rewarding life harvesting, cooking, and tending to his growing family. Kovacs is an avid whiskey and beer taster and loves to spin elaborate yarns with meaning that people will, hopefully, enjoy.

www.ingramcontent.com/pod-product-compliance
Lightning Source LLC
Chambersburg PA
CBHW071155300726
48975CB00004B/1170